Timeless Poetry Anthology

Francis S Cheng, Ph.D.,D.Sc.

Acknowledgement

I am deeply indebted to the encouragement of many published poets at FAXON Poetry Club. Their kind suggestions provided fresh ideas for me to write poems on health, science, and nature.

I am most grateful to Marcia Lewis, former Faxon manager, for introducing me to the Faxon Poetry Club.

My sincere thanks to editors Steve Olechna, June Mandelkern and advisors: JoAnne Bauer, Pamela Guinan, Camilla Hynes, Cheryl Hale, Christopher Jay, Andy Weil, Dave Mello, Dave May, Andrew Hook, Ray Marafino, and Krishna Parthasarathy for their dedication in reviewing anthologies throughout the Perspectives chapbooks publications.

Appreciation is also extended to Graphic artists John Hsu, and Barry Liu, for perfecting the cover designs, and to Hon. Tom Nicotera and Prof. Tsoung Lee for advice on poetry enrichments.

Lastly but not the least, my sincere thanks to lovely wife, Jean, who endured unexpected torment when I had contracted cancer, that nearly obliterated hope and support for children.

Jean took sole responsibility for bread and butter, in restoring the normalcy.

My gratitude to all beloved friends, to my lovely wife and family, remains.

Table of Contents

Timeless Poetry
Anthology

Harbinger of spring

Daffodil pageant welcomes spring –
Stately poised golden buglers, salute
majestic season.
Beaming sun embraces spring charm.

Golden daffodils verge on shore cliff,
overlooking, the surging tides.
Blast bugles with surreal tunes;
Sea breeze caresses golden hues.

Spring revives barren lands.
Helping farmers thaw the mounds,
Tilling sowing with fervent heart.
Longing seedlings burst new life.

Golden daffodil lights torch of spring –
Injects fresh energy kindling life.
Nature unfurls welcome banner.
Spring ventures while great earth nurtures.

Four Seasons for Country Boy

Little boy braves cool spring,

venturing outside with running nose.

Chasing butterflies in prairie,

tumbling over with bloody nose.

Foggy dawning heralds muggy summer.

Golden retriever chases red foxes.

Little boy jumps on pony back,

suffering free fall with black eyes.

Golden foliage outshines azure skyline,

Taking hayride through pumpkin patch.

Golden eagle soaring high,

geese, heading south, wave goodbye.

Drab pumpkin vines litter on farm.

Snow brushes terrain into gleaming plains.

Milking cows rush into cold barn,

flute boy keeps shaking herd calm.

Missing Bulbs

Tulip bulbs sheared
like headless poles.
Pleading for care,
sad looking, standing tall.

Shamrock Holm was puzzled:
Too many animals poked through,
Appeared serrated, with muzzle,
but missing foot prints clue.

Tulips give us pleasant view,
relishes for animal chew.

Tulips, tulips, you're cute,
Displaying beauty unique way.
Few can match elegant view,
Few can match elegant view.

Rushing Tides

Rambling sound paces with roiling waves,

Spring tides smash at unyielding bank.

Being pushed back, keep roaring back.

Stealthy Neap tides creep into Sound,

sweeping victim drown under.

Neaps are puzzling due to similar high and low tides.

Moon's location is perpendicular to Earth-Sun lineup.

Neap tides rise twice at 6 A.M. and 6 P.M.

Spring tides roar high in New (dark), and

full moon (second) quarters.

Neap tides turn somber in

first, and last (third) quarters.

New moon follows identical rising,

setting, times with the Sun.

First quarter moon: rises at noon, sets at midnight.

Second quarter (full) moon: rises at sunset,

sets at sunrise,

Last quarter moon: rises at midnight, sets at noon.

Seagulls brave howling tides,

hovering over waves for seafood pies.

Railroad

Express train smooches meandering rail track,

Chasing distant track toward crescent moon.

Beaming moon blesses embracing lovers,

rushing through whooshing dark tunnels.

Wherever train goes, track ushers ahead:

Crossing the river,

through the mountain,

leading to new frontier.

Ducks on river summersault

against ripples of waves,

Patchy clouds atop mountain

glance at tooting train.

Ground hogs rush into tunnel.

Lover's dream basks in limelight

of crescent arms.

Osteoporosis

Beneath pretty skin there is bone,
even bone is strong it may be gone.
As hormone nourishes bone,
bone care needs be honed.

Bone mass needs grow and care,
for young and dare.
If one squanders timely care,
porous bone becomes nightmare.

One becomes infirm as body ages,
lack of exercise is like bird in cage.
Longing for surfing above wind,
Only sigh for missing nimble wings.

Bone mass is key to staying young,
Build bone mass as we can.
Calcium and vitamins with walking regime,
will keep body healthy without fuss.

Snow Angel

Snow angel dresses in white,
frolicking in midair,
Looking for sweet home on land.

White angel lands on ground.
Sadly she hits water pond.

Bewitched angel can't return
to heavenly paradise.
She is grounded without fun.

Lovely angel hopes, some day,
she will be set free.
But she has to change form to ascend.

She wants to flee with sailing clouds.
Breeze may lend a hand.
But she wants a big lift now.

Missing Whim

Falling rose spirals down,
hitting creek, causing
eddies in a stream.

Pretty rose, waiting for date,
missing loving care bee,
sailing aimlessly in cold stream.

Blooming rose is like
first quarter moon --
Charmingly pretty.

Fully blown rose is
at her prime, full moon --
Jewel crown of princess.

Fading rose is at her

last quarter moon,

little chance for pageant whim.

Falling rose has a wish.

She needs a flower girl,

giving her gentle touch.

Spectacular of St. John River

Influx of St. John River into
Bay of Fundy creates nature's wonder:
of river reflux at Atlantic shore between
New Brunswick and Nova Scotia.

At high tide, torrent river water is
refluxed by roaring tides of
Atlantic Ocean.

Spectacular splash of 25-foot tides,
rivals legendary tsunami cyclones.

Kayak racers sport summersault
at waves' mercy. Brave anglers
are undaunted to ride on
ice-capped waves.

Singing skylarks soar high
to enjoy bird-eye view.
Zipping swallows swoop down,
racing toward turbulent sea.

Century old church tower
continues chiming hymns
for old city of Canada.

Unremitting Passage of Time

Iridescent morning rays punctured
curtain of new dawn.

Shifting shadows gauged passing
moment of our day, until silhouette
flickered against dusk backdrop.

Night crawlers held concert under
moonlight.
Hooting owl lurked in woods
like specter in hunt.

Overnight night bash was only
memory of the past.

Cherry Blossom

Spring breeze caresses blooming cherry.

Tender petals charmingly flutter,

greeting passerby, who

savors nature's charm.

Lovers melt under blooming shade.

Dissolve in cloud,

Feeling bliss in their arms,

expecting the unexpected.

White swans sail in the lake,

loyal escorts for lovers,

witnessing lovers' affair,

keeping in calm silence.

Life Cycle: Bitter, Sweet and Sour

Life cycle of living things for creatures,

or plants alike,

is bound by the nature's metabolic roulette:

bitter beginning, sweet bliss peak, and sour end.

The bitter beginning involves painstaking gestation,

learning from the wild and struggling to avoid

being trapped by unaffordable Vanity Fair:

Like pungent peppers are fatal to innocent toddler.

Sweet adolescence comes with romantic bliss,

and ambitious goals in the prime time of life.

Imaging blossoming apple, pear, and berry trees

are flaunting their juicy sweet fruits at season's peak.

Once peak is over, the nature turns sour on our body.
The stem cell can no longer replenish catalytic
aging of metabolic slowdown: The cells are losing
effectiveness in fending off diseases.

At the end, foods nutrients can't be digested
for energy needs by aging body. When metabolism
slows down, immune system weakens, causing
geriatric sufferings, and illness prone.

Trans Fat
– No Room for Metabolism

Trans fat is not good for energy diet.

New fat was invented in 1910,

for making stale free, long shelf life oil.

It was most popular oil on market in 1950.

People flocked over fast food-chains, and

grocery stores, for trans fat oil -- partially

hydrogenated mono- or polyunsaturated oil.

Vegetable oil has mono- and polyunsaturated molecules,

which get stale odor or discolored after open seals.

Trans fat oil is product of hydrogenated unsaturated oil.

Anti-oxygen, unsaturated oil becomes inert fatty acid.

Trans fat molecule is saturated, with zigzag-structure.

It is good for making margarine or soap to last.

Body enzymes can't metabolize it for energy needs.

Tans fat increases LDL and triglyceride levels.

Mood Reflection

When Anne Mary is happy,

her voice is high.

When she is down, her voice is low.

Listening to her tune,

sense her inner hue.

Anne Mary missed her audition:

Wrong time.

Glee club friends did not come,

she really looked glum.

She tried to hum,

her lips stayed numb.

Fireflies

Fireflies light night sky.
Blinking and glowing make people delight.

Tell me who you are?
Angel of heavenly lights, or
beetle of larva's disguise.

Show me the marvel of luminescent lights,
saving people in your short span of life.

You never stop glowing in your life:
Your light helps stop cancer's might.

Gift of Life – Memory

Spelling bees sound off their enormous memory power.
Memory enriches our life in humanity,
health, learning, sports, and entertainments.

Pundit is judged by his know-how and experience to
advise people for most coveted projects.
His profound memory provides visionary viewpoints.

Memory can never be stolen from brain.
It obliterates images by aging or mentally ill.
Oxygen supplies to brain is critical for memory.

Kilobyte memory creates words,
Mega-byte memory makes audio music,
Gega-byte memory displays video pictures.
Memory is key to healthy living and progress.

Floating Cloud

Floating cloud dawdled in blue sky,
wondering her whereabouts.
When she danced with breeze,
she unfurled her sheen fleece.
She loved to dress in blue when seeking clues.
When dressing in red, she was facing ominous dread.

In the midst of pitch-dark sky,
she was forced by low pressure into
destructive cumulonimbus cloud,
twirled like fleeing eel,
as severe tornado tossed her up,
with whooshing cry.

She was soaked and gross.
She got back in shape by shedding water off,
dousing on great earth.

She made her proud,
helping farmers relieve drought.

Loving Care, Unsung Hero – Water

Very few people questioned my age, since
I came to being 4 billion years ago.

Being part of planet glaciers, I had magic power
of transforming from solid to liquid to vapor phase
in rescuing disastrous planet earth.

Prehistorically,
my mission was extinguishing sprawling infernos,
caused by wild volcanic eruptions.
I sailed on clouds guided by lightning to douse
on earth, threatened by ear-shattering thunders.

My heat preserving power saved zillion lives for
incubating their fetuses. I witnessed the
emerging and extinction of dinosaur rampages
during glacial epoch.

People utilized my phase-change dynamics
to develop drugs, raw materials, hydro powers,
foods, mass transports, for saving lives.

Polluting water and air hurts body enzymes,
which fight infectious diseases to stay healthy.

Surreal Memory – A Dream

A dream creeps up when falling asleep.
No one can expect what comes across:
comic, jovial, romantic or scary clips.

Dreaming means unveiling surreal memory,
privileged for warm-blood animals, but for
cold-blood reptiles have few episodes.

Dream may mix up timing and protagonist in strange way.
Grandpa may dream about childhood experiences,
but kid seldom dreams about future life.

Dream is surrealistic memory surfaced from past scenes:
Triggering dream-walk, yelling, kicking,
even paw-scrapping, or barking, for dozing dog.

Dream never casts a shadow, just sailing through
like apparition. Dreaming is evidence of body
stress due to fever, anxiety, or insomnia.

Tribute to Mother Earth

Dear mother Earth, you are the diva of Universe.

Day-in-day-out, you toil like restless nurse.

The more babies you rear,

the heavier burden you bear.

Your clock ushers new lives to grow,

but none can stop destined flow.

When evils make you fret, you swallow all upsets.

Until you droop bloody lava, we all run for cover.

When you bobble in your course,

We hobble for no repose.

Dedicating your life in nurturing lives,

but disregarding your own tattered mantle.

Dear Mother Earth,

Please don't go!

Our survival has no recourse.

Angel Heart

Angel heart, you are so remarkable:
You pump blood one hundred thousand times a day,
Thirty eight million times a year,
Three billion times in 80-year life span.
But you are hardly been appreciated.

Your role is to support life without bias.
You try hard to beat seventy-two times a minute, non-stop,
until your momentum is hindered.

You bear all the sufferings caused by master's
infatuated drinking and eating habits.
Once blood is contaminated, your chance of
suffering arrhythmia multiplies.

You are the universal symbol of love, courage,
unselfishness with everlasting perseverance.
You make whole planet lively and gallant.

Power of Spectral Waves

Living with invisible spectra is not unthinkable but real:
Sounds of music, TV shows, smart phones, satellite photos,
X-ray for mammograms, MRI for medical diagnostics, IR for
heating, UV for incubator.

Pulsating waves become indispensable tools for
entertainment, healthcare, automation,
and modern comfort.

Invisible spectrum comes alive when power switch is on.
Lack of power, genie spectrum goes to sleep.

Invisible viruses are harmful to human beings.
UV and IR radiations from the sun may stop viruses,
but over exposure causes aging and skin cancer.

Our body generates infrared spectrum to keep body
enzymes active. Even cowherd generates
much heat to keep the stable warm in winter.

Shadow

You gaze at me,

Follow me day and night.

Are you the apparition or angel?

You never speak to me,

nor show affection.

I try to embrace you, but shy away.

When I stretch, you emulate.

Stooped silhouette shows aging body.

Dazzling light makes you shy.

You hides under my heels at high noon.

You stretch like lanky pole at sunset.

Window of Soul – The Eyes

Everyone owns beautiful eyes for perceiving light,

to tell us day from night, revealing mood of low or high.

When happy, eyes are sparkling bright,

When sad, the red drooping eyes shed dejecting light.

Not only the friendly eyes transmit information,

but also displaying instant beam of delight.

Poorly lit light bothers our eyes.

Cataract and glaucoma cost our sight.

Be sure to protect eyes, or streetlights

turn into light-pole mines, when losing sight.

Carrot Paddler – Parrot

Perching parrot looks like carrot.

Orange babbler beats auctioneer.

High-wired walker mimics a joker.

Never fear of height, just glides.

Never feel lonely even alone.

Cruising up and down guarding carrot stand.

You can mimic all you want,

But don't forget what you learn.

When I holler, you soon follow.

What you chirp I don't know.

If I mimic your language,

Soon you retort with the garbage.

Be careful with your orange body.

Never rush into carrot stalks.

You're the best carrot guard,

Don't fall victim of salad bar.

Golden Daisies

Beaming daisies full of charm,

defying the summer heat and burn.

They follow the sun so lively,

as if ladies are dancing gracefully.

Seedlings open eyes in early spring.

They are flimsy and yearning.

Neither birds nor bugs pay a visit,

only the sun and dew care to nourish.

Seedlings grow into summer plants,

Blooming golden crowns cause squirrel frowns.

Birds and bees are noisy haunts –

Shuttling between the golden crowns.

Few posh daisies ever last long,

When snow blizzard hits, they are gone.

Roots are buried under snow pile.

Only the spring sun ushers their return.

Blizzard

Mother nature is never settled.
Her revolving motion changes weather patterns,
befuddling living critters.

At blizzard, bare trees, bushes, and verdant pines
were transformed into brilliant magic kingdom
of decorative snow confetti, rivaling sparkling spring scenes.

Starving seagulls hovered over white velvet mounds,
seeking food. Raccoons tipped over garbage cans
littered with booty and spoors.

Life became miserable without power
and water, as if back to cave living.

Mother nature might be broken hearted!

Parting Foliage

Being planted together, and grew outdoors
with elegant spring blossom.

Reminiscing the joy of frolicking with bees,
and being caressed by soothing breeze.
Surviving the searing heat of summer,
and inclement blitz of storms.

The blissful life is soon drawing to an end,
like ephemeral carnation.

Vivid green color is fading, foliage are
dressed in fall suits, appearing
more mature and revered,
but less certain for future.

Whispering to their peers with prayers
in the twilight, hoping none will ever part
without bidding goodbye.

Swan

White swan glides on blue lake.
Water mirrors majestic image.

Baths in caressing breeze,
Dangled worry ripples away.

Blue lake is marred by industrial discharges.
Never can fathom damage to shellfish.
Hollow shells litter by lakeside.

Muting is song sung.
But is herald of clean Nature.
Never treat like abject wildfowl.

Frozen Estuary

Deep freeze defaces estuary into glaciers.
Pleasure boats, steamers are out of sight.

Motionless ducklings packed
by the shore, droop, hushed.

Morning sun gently caresses the lifeless flock,
enlivens all quacking angels.

Mother's Day

We are grateful to mother's love
and sacrifice for her children.
Even if we are not with mom,
We love to celebrate mother's day.

Universe would be vacuum without
Mother Earth. Whole world would be
chaotic without mother lands. Country would
move backward without mother's love.

Dandelion

Dandelion shows off in early spring --
aggressive, fast-grown, wild weed.
Flaunting itself with brilliant yellow florets,
which puff like silvery fireworks.

Puffing pap-pus carries achenes like
paratroopers filling the air.
Bristling pap-pus looks pretty, but may
make people sneezing badly.

Ruminant cow and goat don't
care about dandelion.
They prefer relish grass
to bitter wild weed.

Larvae of butterfly and moth feed on
dandelion roots for surviving.
Cultivated dandelion is good antioxidant,
and diuretic for heat exhaustion.

Bamboo

Bamboo sways in the wind,
gently, it never breaks by storm.
Green leaves extend like fins.

Bamboo sways in the wind,
Regardless of how you try to win,
It just swings in gentle form.

Bamboo sways in the wind,
Gently, it never breaks by storm.

Back Safety

Back injury causes lifetime misery.
It saps annual healthcare revenue
ten billion like sinkhole.

Back injuries come from lifting, falling,
pushing, tumbling, and carrying.

People should avoid heavy lifting.
Don't be a superman!
Avoid lifting very heavy load
beyond one's strength.

Never twist waist while lifting,
or shoveling wet snow.
Do not work in confined space with
contorted posture.

Don't sit or stand for too long.
It is very hard on lower back.

Always use legs for lifting.
Avoid falling – using cart
or dolly for moving.

Constantly exercise the back:
Stand with back against a wall. Raising
legs to strengthen back and hip muscles.

Magnolia

Blooming pink magnolia,
dot along meandered river,
displaying conspicuous charms,
swinging with breezes.

Elegant florets are fragile,
like ephemeral cicadas,
crying during sunset.
Beauty is just a blip.

Florets seek affection before
fading. Breezes caress
them and blowing away.
Stream kisses while sending off.

Overcoming the odds,
Magnolia comes back for
spring pageant. Even life is short,
memory lingers.

Sky

Sky is hollow sphere, shrouded by air.

Water forms clouds, masking azure view.

Spring shower pours, kids race out like hares.

Nature pulls prank, none can find clue.

Carrousel earth is powerful, but uncertainties rumble.

Even in hot summer, flu and disease get rampant.

Amidst life's vulnerability, learn how to care.

Constant exercise promotes healthy life.

Once air is gone, azure sky loses its view.

As high pressure returns, sky greets azure hue.

Invisible dust particles reflect light for color and hue..

Lack of moisture causes draught to linger.

All sky spectaculars are from air and water.

Temperature and pressure affect air currents and weather patterns.

Pollutions add to nature's miseries.

Rampant diseases are due to contaminated enzymes.

Protein and Fat

It is difficult to choose between juicy steak burger,
and large fries plus coke for lunch on the go.
Steak burger has high protein and starch, while
fries and coke have high fat and sugar.

Protein stake tastes like meat tenderizer,
but when burnt, it smells like fertilizer.
Fries become crunchy, when burnt,
Never smell rotten, even charred.

Human body is composed of protein and fat in balance.
When off balanced, body shape skewed or bulged.
Proteins are reactive toward acid and base.
Stem cell is protein with enormous growth power.

No one likes cancer, which acts sneaky.
Cancer is protein enzyme attacking fatty tissue.
Cancer always pops up in tender areas:
at prostate, breast, lung, pancreas, and womb.

Leadership

Five fingers decide to compete for leadership facing a judge.

Thumb finger asserts: Rule of thumb is my trademark.
I should be voted for leadership.

Index finger argues:
I point the way for you guys to follow.
You will be lost without me.

Middle finger says:
I stand tall to represent all of you.
I am impartial,
flaunting with ring of freedom and love.

Ring finger retorts: I am the most trusted one.
Wedding couples need me to prove their loving care for life.

Pinky finger smiles: Look, if I am gone, you guys lose most grip-power to climb and lift like disabled.

Judge declares:

You guys are melting pot; everybody is great leader.

Let work together to achieve wonders.

Geriatric Destiny

Doctor relies on chart, lest judging wrong.

Plastic surgery turns geriatric into bridal face.

Botox injection lifts wrinkles but not for long.

Stores refuse senior discount sans I.D.

Senior wants to stay young and healthy.

Cosmetic maker gets lucky.

Even best anti-aging creams

can't revive happy dreams.

Beautiful gaits turn into dragging hate.

Outdoor jogging creeps into tea sipping.

Gossiping!

Willpower wanders away from fate.

Destiny is intriguing odyssey of life.

Life is adventure in perspective.

Geriatric destiny is invisible usher.

Life strives, when destiny drives.

Summer Solstice

June is most charming, festive month,
when solstice rewards newlyweds
with ever happy honeymoon.

Longest day at solstice, when red sun gazes high,
while moon slips low near horizon,
enchanting image looms.

Millennial hold midnight bash at solstice,
then falling asleep in no time.
But grandparents endure insomnia,
searching for Sominex.

June is most pleasant, perfect month
for great activities. People names
after June deserves best deference in life.

Bewildered Nature

Sudden burst of spring in midwinter kindled
high spirit for chirping cardinals.
Charming cadence, bobbing, from limb to twig,
competing with crows' noisy band.

Hungry squirrels chased after bird feeder,
hanging under tree in mid air.
Somersaulting on twigs as stunt.
Flicking foliage undulated like confetti.

Sparrows started mating under eaves,
Annoyed by chipmunks' hide and seek.
Shifting site to gutter end,
Suffering bad luck on heavy rain.

Pleasant morning reverted to frigid night.
People hid inside, enjoying fireplace.
But creatures survived in severe cold,
shivering in wild until sun rises.

Treasure of Gifted Body

Body is parental gift of hope and legacy.

Body and mind are inseparable.

Body is tangible; mind is unfathomable.

Mind dictates body's action.

Enchanting world seduces body, with surreal fantasy.

Mind makes decisions; brain takes note.

Body obeys the commands.

Mind's loss makes body aimless ricochet.

Brain has hormone, melatonin, to control

insomnia, and prevents vision loss.

Body needs foods and vitamins to

protect DNA and genetic functions.

Adrenal hormones affect blood pressure,

weight changes and kidney functions.

Pituitary hormones control thyroid

immune systems, and body pains.

Squirrel

Squirrel is nimble, mimicking, yet short memory.

Nests are found on ground, hollow trunk, or limbs.

Squirrel plays on tree, racing on power line,

like no brainer.

But it stumbles on highway, worse than deer.

Squirrel calls like high-pitch songbird.

They build bulk leaf nest on limbs,

or den in tree cavity.

Often squirrel ventured into hollowed knurl,

beaten back by screeching owl.

Squirrel works hard to overcome short memory.

Keeping nuts mouthful in cheek pouches and hands,

Racing home before lost in land.

Sharing meals with cubs for joy.

Squirrel does not hoard with large stock.

Gig economy is a way to go.

Enjoy handy booty from birdseed raids.

When snowstorm hits, just go hibernate in cold.

Bird in Scorching Summer

People survive heat with air conditioners.

Bird stays alive with tree shelter.

Scorching heat kindles forest fire.

Cruel fire becomes bird's nightmare.

People check body temperature.

Bird endures trapped heat torture.

High blood pressure is bad for human.

Yet, avian endures high stress to fly.

Bird has no means to fend of high heat.

It suffers heat stroke above 115 degrees.

Desert bird is rarely seen.

Only vulture cruises for meat.

Fatality is high for avian species.

Living in wild, fighting for food and water.

Nature's challenge is severe without shelter.

Bird can't shed tears but appears dear.

Father's Day

Father's day is upon us.

But there is none for birds.

Two busy birds take turn in

regurgitating for hungry chicks.

How skillful is chick feeding!

Parent bird regurgitates on wiggling chicks,

without being confused on particular one.

All chicks look healthy and ready to run.

Father's day is special holiday for dad.

But it is not national holiday for kids and mom.

Blissful holiday showed off credit cards.

Only way to cut debt is working double hard.

Father's day is for privileged human beings.

Even pets are not allowed,

because they are fixed.

Only gift allowed is pet chow.

Seeing-Eye Dog

Teenager Keith was blind at birth.

Shepherd dog, Sammy, lent his sight.

Sammy took Keith to school,

holding together like brothers.

When Keith and Sammy crossed the street,

Sammy's heartbeat started to race.

But remained discreet,

lest Keith turned visceral fear of trauma.

Keith cuddled with Sammy

by street corner.

Sammy made sure Keith stayed

warm and safe like nanny.

When Sammy became hungry,

nudging at Keith's thigh.

But never got fury,

only whining cry.

Moonlit Beach

Strolling on moonlit beach
Unsettling mind roiled by surfing tides.
Soothing breeze can't offer for ride.
Swooping swallows greet you,

Strolling with hunched grandpa, as kid,
holding his cane for support and comfort.
Stroke had crippled his arm and leg.
His shadow balled up like mushroom.

Moonlight evokes pensive feeling.
Ancestors and parents are memorable history.
Ask the moon what shall I be?
Roaring tides gave poignant reply.

Strolling on moonlit beach,
watching twinkling stars.
Jupiter and Venus in west sky,
Superlative beauty of universe
greets stars in tranquility.

An Ode to Air

Lost friend,

lonely,

ailing and despaired.

Air is lifeline!

It makes healthy life,

keeps Earth lit and

habitable for creatures.

Air is unappreciated.

It provides oxygen, but

harbors bacteria and pollutants.

Airwave makes lovely melody,

helping communication and

seeing twinkling stars in Milky Way.

Without air,

life disappears.

Time – Marker of History

Time sails as Earth turns.

It comes quietly, no one runs.

She is the angel of hope,

healer of suffering,

and justice of destiny.

Time is cradle for the young,

golden nugget for the mid-aged,

and witness for the old.

When you are happy, time adds zest to your joy.

When you are sad, time offers you a reprieve.

Time sails for history making.

Life flows with social tides.

Time never shows sign of decay.

While life glitters like morning dews.

Lonely Angler

Diving sea gar showed no shadow in water,
evading angler's watchful eyes.

When gar bobbed its head,
angler saw rising bubbles.
Even gar dove quickly,
churning eddies rippled.

Lonely angler reeled alone,
hovering seagull staying high.

Glaring sunset sailed along,
Angler's shadow was never gone.

Rainbow Trellis

Scorching sun burned tomato plants,
turning greens into drab stumps.

Using perforated garden hose
to spray the garden against rising sun.

All in sudden, fine mist spurted from the hose,
turned into iridescent rainbow trellises,
as if angel's mural.

Cardinals, sparrows and wrens
flocked to perch on mirage trellis,
gotten somersaulted and cold showers.

Only earthworms got saved from
burning ground for seeking shelter.

Preferred Drink: Coffee, Tea, or Vanilla?

People show different penchants for drinks.
Herbal flavor varies with coffee, tea or vanilla.
If flavor does not suit you, you blink!
If lukewarm coffee were served, you glare!

Drink has its health benefits and side effects:
Too much coffee stimulates brain, causing insomnia.
Too much tea at meal, robs mineral iron.
Vanilla tastes bland, but lessens allergies.

Coffee, ice tea, and vanilla chocolate are fighting
for No.1 drink on market.
Too much sugary, cold drinks disrupt insulin
and metabolism hastening aging.

Vanilla ice cream may not be as popular
as chocolate cousin.
Health effect of vanilla extract is much better
In coping with anxiety and fever.

Revolving Earth

Mother Earth impels herself to revolve,
nurturing hungry creatures on back.
Motion creates winds, refreshing air
and water without short cut.

Motion is secret of lasting health.
Million DNA cells replicate every hour.
Heart never stops rumbling,
as mind flashes boggling signs.

Foods and drugs appear lifeless outside.
Inside molecules are earnestly
swinging with water molecules
for freshness.

Mother Earth – Most trusted role model.
Sadly, few follow her exercise deeds.
Creatures succumb before her,
betrayed by robotic luxuries.

Remarkable skin

Skin gives boundary and sentry for life.
None can survive without.
Beautiful skin displays life's prime,
Callous skin reveals life's ultimate trait.

Skin is never meant for beauty contest.
Skin responds to fever and sensing danger –
bulging eyelids reveal insomnia trouble,
hepatitis stains skin to yellow.

Skin contains three layers of epidermis,
dermis, and subcutaneous composite.
Fibrillose collagen protein helps bone
and muscle join together.
Elastin is protein maintaining skin elasticity.

Enzymes on skin remove dead keratin protein.
Vivid tattoo ink and pigment, may impede
enzymes causing skin cells to fade prematurely.

Sweet Tooth

Spring is ushered by blooming cherries.

Yellow daffodil follows suit.

Butterflies and bees bob busily.

Never know if they're happy.

Azure sky contrasts verdant ground.

Kids are busy running around.

Candies and cookies in their hands,

Mouthful keeps them slowing down.

Sugar causes craving for sweet tooth.

Sugar is made of glucose and fructose joined together.

Fructose leads at sweetness race,

But glucose is energy ace.

Sweet tooth causes decay, and root canal.

High blood sugar leads to obesity,

cognition, and heart diseases.

Worries, but never be final.

Nasty Influenza (Flu)

Inclement weather and flu turn people blue.

Flu spreads via saliva or mucus from mouth and nose.

Viruses cling to skin and lung without clue.

Preying on enzymes as pack of wolves.

Virus deprives host energies –

Using sialylated enzyme,

with N-acetylneuraminic acid, (glucosylamino acid),

to lure body enzymes, helping virus cloning.

Host suffers fever; cough, with running red nose.

Over the counter, medicines parade at stores.

Flu viruses get free ride from victims,

traveling around the world.

Medicine is toxic to virus and human, avoids overdose.

Sanitized napkins contain ethyl alcohol.

Flu virus enzyme has plenty of alcohol outer-shield,

undaunted by sanitization.

Using diluted vinegar, for salad dressing,

to wipe off saliva or mucus from hands or nose,

may be more effective to stop virus spreading.

Epidermis – Outer Skin

Skin is not for looking pretty.
It has three vital layers
in revealing organ illness –
swelling, yellowing, and dark spots.

Skin defines boundary of body.
Organs are homeless without skin.
Skin breathes, absorbs, perspires,
and exchanges info with brain.

Young skin flaunts radiance,
Resilient charms like roses.
Aging skin glints with wrinkles,
Varicose veins twist like old pine.

Skin has ability to heal, and lessens
body's salt content.
Perspiration on daily walks
helps lower blood pressure
and improves heart health.

Deep Freeze

Winter freezes:

Barren lands,

nakedly frozen trees.

Why torment dormant greens?

Allowing creatures warmly clad.

No one knows,

Nature's whim.

April Shower

April shower frees Mother Earth
from winter shackle.
Refreshing shower revives
her shattered hope.

Great Earth nourishes
creatures in her cradle.
Taking heavy tolls from hurricanes,
tornados and forest fires.

Aging Earth is stripped of powerful tools
in preventing natural disasters.
Untimely rainfall and draught ruin seasonal
crops, aggravated by pollutions.

April shower is big relief for great Earth,
but not enough to cure nature's ill:
Fever on the ground,
dizzy spells in the air.

Nature's Beauty

Gazing at beautiful sunrise,
hovering eagles over Niagara fall.
Blazing sunset triggers pleasant
appreciation of nature's beauty.

Dazzling torrents, colorful foliage,
shuttling gulls, and tourists mingle
in spectacular view.

Camera clicking, meeting friends,
souvenirs hunting, and hiking
in fresh air make people relaxed and happy.

Nature's aesthetic simplicity,
and motion in harmony is
her way of lasting longevity.

Elapsing Prime

Fresh perfume worn out over night;
Beautiful flowers wilted in weeks.

Brief living cicadas shrilled before demise.
Pageant beauty became mid-aged lady.
Grand parents left their legacy with mercy.

Who could enjoy ever-lasting bliss in life?
Life's best chance was at prime age.
Never indulged in passionate binge
before liver enzymes were ruined.

Mosquitoes

Blooming forsythia greets sparkling spring.

Mild weather incubates larvae in swamp.

No sooner they are hatched, than

metamorphosed into bloodthirsty mosquitoes.

Mosquitoes are attracted to carbon dioxide

for warmth and blood seeking.

Blood sucking vampires may carry diseases,

spreading freely by preying

on animals, birds, fowls, and people.

Mosquitoes stay on water without worrying

about being drowned.

The pests frustrate people with rumbling

threat of seeking blood debt.

Only way to cope with annoying pests

is to keep any water spot alkaline with baking soda,

adding a few drops of detergents

to drown larvae and insects.

Purpose of Plastics

Plastics are meant to save forestry,

and benefit human beings.

The overcapacity of utility plastics,

and less recycling facilities cause

land filled scraps to become sea drifted wastes.

Most popular plastic septuplets shape our way of life.

For recycling numbers are:

No.1, PET (Polyethylene terephthalate) for water, soft drinks bottles.

Cigarette filters. Low toxicity, flammable, melts at 250C.

No.2, HDPE (High density polyethylene) for milk jugs, detergent

and vinegar bottles. Low toxicity, flammable, melts at 150C.

No.3, PVC (Polyvinyl chloride) for squeezable shampoo bottles, dry

food containers, and fast food service trays. It releases toxic chlorine

when ignited.

It burns but self extinguishing, melts at 125C.

No.4, LDPE (Low density polyethylene) for grocery bags, shrink wrapping. Degradable when exposed to the sun and UV, low toxicity, melts at 90C.

No.5, PP (Polypropylene) for yogurt cups, straws, and syrup bottles and caps.
Low toxicity, flammable, melts at 160C.

No.6, PS (Polystyrene) for foams for packaging, hot drink cups, meat trays,
electronics packaging and insulation. Sun and UV resistance, never degrades,
Easily burns with black soot.

No.7, Nylon 66 (Hexamethylenediamine and adipic acid) for fashion fabrics, sporting goods and fishing gears. High strength, tear resistance, will not burn easily, melts at 268C.

Others plastics like silicone implants, pace makers, hearing aids, automobile, and medical instruments, are made from other plastics.

Spring Storm

Unexpected spring storm in May changed
landscape of coastal cities.
Rumbling torrent drowned the towns,
turned streets into uncharted rivers.

Rain and wind unmercifully pounded
on victims – carrying crying baby and kids,
fleeing submerged houses on canoes.

Whining puppies clung to Johnny's backpack,
drenched and trembling.
Johnny was shaken and hungry,
struggling to calm his pet.

People returned home after disaster.
Sadly, basement turned into pool.
Floating furniture drifted like boat,
only saving little mouse's life.

Soybean and Corn

Soybean and corn grow in spring –
Vivid green, silky waves ripple under glaring sun.
Breeze caresses fresh crops, feeding the world,
framer's dream.

Soybean and corn grow on farm.
Each crop treasures its own value.
Soybean shows off her protein pods,
Corn wraps her ears for energy.

Tasteless soybean makes people
lean, robust;
Sweet corn infuses starch,
plump.

Soybean turns into soymilk, tofu,

veggie burgers,

low in fat and calories,

with Omeg-3 and protein.

Corn is rich in natural sugar and carbohydrates,

containing Omega-6, Vitamins B1, calcium and iron.

Too much corn or popcorn makes people plump.

Keeping moderate consumption to stay healthy.

Habit

A habit can be good or bad,
No one knows its effect.

When one suffers a pruritic scalp,
His fingers relentlessly chase after it,
Habitually!

Scratching causes contagious
itching effect over the skull.
Worse yet, bacteria from hands and nails
start to cause skin infections.

Itching sensation is hard to stop like sneezing.
Only hot water may soothe its discomfort.
Zinc oxide helps stop itching with healing.

Etiolated Plant and Vegetable

Plant and vegetable get sick also.

Their health is affected by cold weather,

rainfall, drought and soil quality.

They suffer etiolated diseases

when they are in deficiency of nitrogen,

potassium, and phosphorus.

Nitrogen (N) deficiency causes poor plant growth:

Leaves turn pale green or yellow.

Often happens to vegetables like cabbage.

Rye grass green manure helps nitrogen from leaching out.

Potassium (K) deficiency affects fruits and vegetables,

like potatoes, tomatoes, apples,

currants and gooseberries.

Symptoms are brown scorching,

curling of leaf tips, and

yellowing with purple spots.

Potassium (K) deficient plants are more prone

to frost damage and disease.

For cure: Composted bracken, manure or K-rich fertilizers.

Phosphorus (P) deficiency is most common in high
rainfall area: especially on acidic, clay, or poor chalky soils.
Most susceptible are carrots, lettuce, spinach,
apples, pears, and gooseberries.

Fruits are small and sour tasting.
Abating with rock phosphate or P-rich fertilizers.

Sneezing Misery

Allergy is untidy fad of spring.

Colorful flowers unleash their male pollens.

Like specters frolic in the air.

Ticklish nose flares up like red fruit.

Sneezing echoes squeaky door in the morning.

Allergy is untidy fad of spring.

Using Q-tip moistened with 5%, clear

vinegar, to wipe off nostril, helps

alleviate the sneezing misery.

Fortress of Life

Physical body is living fortress of life.
Few can enjoy life without body.

Body makes life meaningful.
Knowing body is organic trove
for life sustenance -- coveted by
bacteria for cloning paradise.

Nature uses cells to produce life,
control diseases for lasting health.

Everyone is responsible for own
body and good immune system --
Treating foods and drugs as medicines for safety.

Spring Elegance

Winter blizzard in early March
is finally gone, replaced with
tingling cold, snappy breeze.

Mother nature refreshes great earth
with lively panoramic view:
numerous seagulls on beach zoom
eastward against the sun
like dancing silver coins.

Nearby pasture is dotted with snow pile,
While daffodils, and forsythia, are barely waking up.

Frozen stream starts to rumble.
Cardinals and blue jays look for seeds,
in empty bird feeders, rivalling prying squirrels.

Farmers get busy tilling and sowing.
Kids venture outside with kite flying,
bike racing, and dog walking.

Foliage Destiny

Summer heat infused fresh energy for grasses,
plants and trees to restore aesthetic beauty of nature.
Blossomed trees attracted bees
and butterflies bobbing through verdant maze.

As earth tilted, Sun bowed low and its energy sapped.
Greeting new fall, foliage donned
red, yellow-orange suits
for ostentatious parade.

Day became shorter and cold night lingered.
Leaves shriveled, color faded,
starting to fall one after another,
spiraled down.

Drab-brown tattered leaves piled up
on ground, aimlessly tangoed with whirlwind,
making rustling noise, as if dancing
toward vanity destiny.

Allergy Season

Spring embraces nature's beauty
as Mother Earth sports vogue of puberty.
In no time, budding trees, shrubs,
and plants burst forth into full bloom.

Dazzling daylight reflects pristine beauty of blossoms
against backdrop of blue skies.
Busy bees and butterflies are collecting
nectar in the maze of corollas.

Floral petals and pollen sail through breeze
as smog in midair, hoping to land
at carpel of flowers for blind date.

Unknowingly, invisible male-gamete pollens
land at human nostril like pathogens,
which are greeted with histamine immune responses,
causing sneezes and allergy.

Tomorrow

Time never slips past tomorrow.
Tomorrow never ends.
Time wears people out of aging,
tomorrow still comes unfazed.

Bright sun stays aloft in skies,
gazing at Earth, which is
pirouetting with rhythmic daily beats.

Yesterday was past deeds
for reassessment.

Today is true moment
for fulfillment.

Tomorrow is time for reckoning
ultimate milestone.

People never bid goodbye to tomorrow,
but are eager to cherish tomorrow.

Flu Virus Threatens All Ages

Flu virus causes havoc as inclement weather
persists with little relief.
Human immune system could not stop
viral and bacterial infections,
causing fever and pneumonia.

Human body has glycosylsialate,
most important protein,
in our brain and skin for sensing and nerve functions.

Flu Virus uses its pointed-armor arm, polypeptide,
bound to its own sialic acid group,
to confuse human-host immune proteins,
hijacking cells for unchecked replications.

Virus is invisible, contagious protein floating in air.

It is lifeless dust particle,

but rather deadly:

Being able to hijack host enzyme for speedy cloning,

kids and grand baby boomers are most vulnerable.

Flu virus hates hot perspiration and vinegar.

Perspiring body wastes are toxic to virus.

Active and athletic people are less affected by flu.

Using vinegar to clean nostril helps stop sneezing.

Life's Treasure

Great treasure of life is not hidden,
Only it's value rewards quickly but neglected.

Crying baby starts gaping happily
at mother's tender nudge.

Aging parents turn healthier,
when giving good care.

Even drooped houseplant perks up,
when caressed with soft music.

All is 'Love' that has infused
spurting energy for a miracle.

Love is hidden beneath plain color: Sound,
exercising, food, sharing, and working,
as Nature's surviving promise.

Any one may trigger love chemistry

beyond textbook definitions.

Life is beautiful, flimsy flower,

but brilliant and durable, when loving care nourishes.

Wasabi Condiment

When food or condiment is too spicy,
people grimace and turn clownish.

Wasabi is green appetizer for uniquely
minced tuna, eel, shrimp,
and raw fish sushi plates.
Each plate is served with vividly green,
velvet-textured, wasabi condiment.

No sooner you swallow first piece of tuna sushi,
smudged with yummy looking green wasabi,
than your tongue, nose,
and throat burst into burning sensation,
surpassing hot pepper or horseradish.

Don't worry about thirty-second of hot
flush and embarrassment.
People next to you act as much clownish
with frowning, tearing, and rejoicing.

After thirty-second of tormenting moment,
soothing, mild mint let you savor the most
with decay fighting condiment.

Seasonal Garden

Starting garden in cold spring is difficult.

Little hope to germinate beans, cucumbers,

and squashes under threat of frost until late May.

Vivid green sprouts welcome

flourishing new season under caressing breeze.

Hot summer adds life to growing plants,

shooting up like ivies, dotted with red,

yellow, and white flowers, against trellis

for shuttling bees and butterflies.

Thanks to insect matchmakers, fresh beans,

cucumbers, and squashes hang beautifully

like parade of bird feeders.

Fall weather makes plants gloomy:

Beans, cucumbers, and squashes dwindle

and fade with drab vines.

Late Blizzard Eugene

Ground hog saw the shadow,
warm Spring would not follow.
St. Patrick parade was cold,
Blizzard Eugene continued to hold.

Great earth was covered with snow,
tree dressed in white robes.
Robins and orioles had no place to rest,
raccoons sneaked out like pests.

Being buried over ten inches snow,
paralyzed traffics waiting for plow.
Pipe broke stopped water flow,
anxiety caused headache in panic.

Spring fever is catching on,
but cold spell won't let go.
Cold or hot teeters every other day,
outfit changes in funny way.

Powerless: Blackout Storms

Alfred blitzed East Coast.
Streets paralyzed by falling trees.
Cables and power lines twisted
like jungle of black snakes.

Night gripped the darkness.
Howling winds and pelting sleet
swept through nightmarish skies,
as if life in the wild.

Glittering icicles, on trees and bushes,
started to shed tears
before final departure,
demanded by rising sun.

Spoiled foods littered the fridge.
None cared for stale bread
and cold coffee.
Quick fix was McDonald's.

Most Stressful Planet

Mother earth is most stressful planet.

She kept billion creatures alive with big heart,

but suffers unbearable stresses.

Pristine mountains and oceans adorn

her landscapes for soothing agonies within.

Mother earth has suffered chronic ailments of

bloating pressures from magma,

natural gas, and crude oil, trapped under zigzag,

unsettled tectonic plates,

giving impression of secure planet.

Overly exploration of natural resources for oil,

and strategic materials causes excessive tectonic stresses,

surface erosions, and pervasive global pollutions beyond

earth's ability for self remediation.

Moreover, people are threatened by volcanic eruptions, hurricanes, tornados, drought, and flooding.

Natural disasters destroy the ecosystems;
rampant bacteria seek host cells in humans.
Viruses attack mammals and birds in causing plague.

If mother earth perishes,
solar system collapses!
Universe eclipses!

Nature's Harmony

Reticent white swans sail with quacking ducks,
against dazzling, rising sun,
in a glittering estuary.
Seagulls circle above anglers' boats;
Swallows pass through in great hurry.

Array of pines stand like palace guards,
Caressing breeze sweeps green outfits.
Red cardinals shuttle back and forth, playing
with red house finch mistaken for their chicks.

Joggers, hikers, and bikers enjoy fresh air
and morning exercises before office.
Newlyweds set up beach party with fuming grills,
seagulls, squirrels queue for spoils.

Green parakeets build big nests on top of silver maple.
Babbling offbeat sounds until hawk approaches,
Soon sound silences.

Hydrangea

Hydrangea is beloved guardian of ecology.

Its delicate clusters of silky flowers blossom

between July and September with blue,

red, pink, purple, white and cream colors.

Color changes with soil acidity,

and aluminum content in soil.

Acidic soil with pH below 5.0 results in vivid blues;

Neutral soil at pH 7.0 flashes deep pink.

Scientific reports link Alzheimer's disease

to aluminum metal,

which we contact though pots and pans,

beverage cans, antacids, and antiperspirants.

High aluminum in body wreaks havoc on body enzymes.

Aluminum is more available in acidic potting soils,

resulting in blue flowers. Hydrangea tends to

clean up aluminum ions in soils,

regardless of large shrub, or small tree species.

Digital Tennis Game

Tennis game is at its new dawn and fashioned with high tech.
Agile player contrives formidable plot to outsmart seeded players.

New bleed of unranked players tried to unseat
the defending champ from pinnacle of fames tower,
only met with tantalizing despair.

Frustrated young loser knew typical analog power serve would never
outwit super stars except risking with digitally punctuated power serves.

His digitally high tech worked convincingly: Every power serve
hit borderline or tip of baseline.
Old champ was caught flatfooted.

Tennis game is at its new dawn.
New champ is trickily digital lad.

Thimble Islands

Thimble Islands, crown jewels of Long Island Sound,

display sparkling pink granite archipelago landforms --

outcrops of retreating glaciers, 100 to 250 centuries ago.

Panoramic sight of archipelago embraced

by blue horizon of sound, verdant lawns,

and white pines, except thimble black berries.

Stony Creek harbor provides natural sanctuary

for eagles and migrating seals as paradise for wilds.

In 1970 the islands turned private for resorts,

seals were gone ever since.

Victorian and modern mansions rest

on top of thirty visible islets.

Residents enjoy angler's crops,

race boats ricocheting

on high tide, and whispering waves at night.

Pulse of Earth – Time

Who cares about age of time?
Time is 13.7 billion years old, since Universe was created.
Time is the pulse of earth.

Is time relevant to life?
If time stops, sun eclipses.
Life loses air supply
as earth demises.

Time is guardian of life –
Monitor of victors and losers in history –
fair justice to all.

Time is seamless mantle
of Universe. It displays the past,
and mystifies future.

Countless people dream of
time blessing for becoming
twinkling stars in galaxy.

Magnificent Trios
– Moon, Earth, and Sun

Sizzling hot sun radiates iridescent beams on earth,

protect wild lives, identify objects with glaring rays,

cast shadows, and offers heat energy for survival.

Restless earth spins like giddy carrousel,

Inundated with enormous amount of water

for weather moderation, vegetation,

and food chain.

Quite posing moon evokes mood changes

from glee to gloom. Moon is mother of empathy, love, intelligence,

and hope.

Soothing moonlight improve quality of life.

Great artists, musicians and scientists created

their masterpieces under moonlight's blessings.

Bacteria, Viruses, and Enzymes

Human body is full of synchronized linkages of active
protein enzymes with glucose and lipid (fat) nutrients.
Bacteria and viruses love to invade human body
as host to foster cloned viruses causing host to demise.

A virus has RNA and DNA enclosed in protein outer coat,
lifeless parasite. It stays alive after seizing human cells
and injecting RNA and DNA, with toxic protein enzymes.
Causing: influenza, shingles, pneumonia, smallpox, and measles.

A bacterium is much larger than virus, having
complete mono-cell or poly-cell structure.
Gut bacteria help food digestion; Bad bacteria cause E. coli,
strep throat, tuberculosis, salmonella and meningitis.

All proteins have molecular structure of amino acid.
Even bacteria and virus have basic
proteins, like human enzymes.
Drugs help immune system to kill viruses or bacteria
by paralyzing amino or carboxyl group for better cure.

Turtle Snaps Heron

Sizzling heat prompted birds to seek water.
Pond on farm provided relief for geese, ducks,
and wading herons.

Geese, ducks, and herons helped themselves,
without queuing, for frolicking, somersaulting, and diving.
Wading herons were eagerly seeking shellfish
and worms in ebbing pond water.

Farmers took a day off at farmhouse – enjoying keg rums.
Napping after binge, paying no attention to
heron's distress calls.

Not until flapping geese cries and quacking ducks drew
attentions toward fighting between heron chick
and huge, grey snapping turtle.

The bill of little chick was pinned inside turtle's mouth.
Both were tangled in mire.
Injured chick was rescued from turtle's snapping teeth from suffocation.

Glowing Ecliptic Halo

Young boy was hiking on wheelchair along scenic reservoir.
His hands served as pistons and brakes.
He wheeled uphill and downhill with great determination.

Thirsty, exhaustion and fatigue
etched on his face: Bleary eyes, biting lips,
heavy perspiration and soiled hands.

His hands bruised,
reaching for bottle water from fellow walkers.
He said, "Thanks", gasping,
and rolled on with tired hands.

Disease had paralyzed him at early age.
But little angel kept his life normal and exciting.
Wishing this twinkling star would glow ever brighter.

Meaning of Aging

Aging is nature's unique sculpture of life
in transition. It records real-time
physical and emotional deeds.

Seniors are vested with experiences, paid for
with graying and wrinkles. But falling behind
baby protégé in high tech.

Aging is nature's merry-go-round on lives:
Enjoying wild rides while young and carefree;
Turning worrisome while graying and ailing.

Aging is not gloomy omen.
It guides us to change pace
with waning physical health,
Opening up life's new horizon.

INDEX

Timeless Poetry Anthology

作　　者／Francis S. Cheng

封面攝影／John Y Hsu

出版策劃／獵海人

製作銷售／秀威資訊科技股份有限公司

　　　　　114 台北市內湖區瑞光路76巷69號2樓

　　　　　電話：+886-2-2796-3638

　　　　　傳真：+886-2-2796-1377

網路訂購／秀威書店：https://store.showwe.tw

　　　　　博客來網路書店：http://www.books.com.tw

　　　　　三民網路書店：http://www.m.sanmin.com.tw

　　　　　金石堂網路書店：http://www.kingstone.com.tw

　　　　　讀冊生活：http://www.taaze.tw

出版日期／2019年5月

定　　價／NT\$ 250；US\$ 10